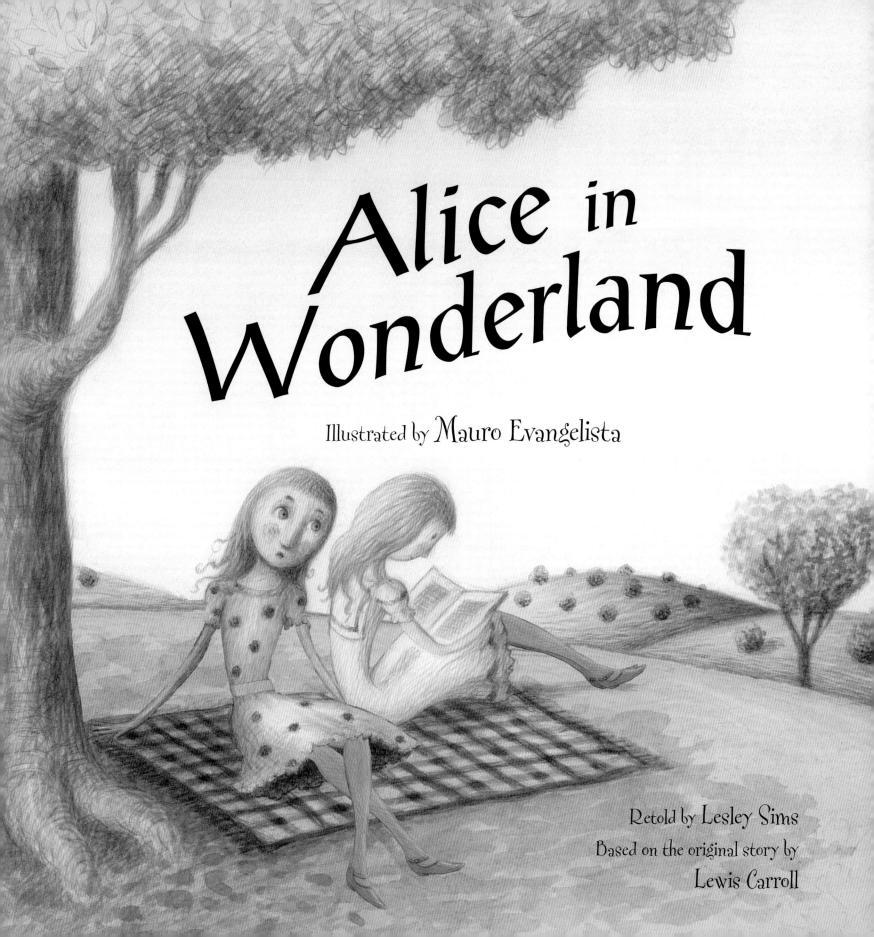

Alice in Wonderland

Illustrated by Mauro Evangelista

Retold by Lesley Sims
Based on the original story by
Lewis Carroll

Alice's sister was deep in her book
and Alice was feeling bored.

All at once, she saw a
White Rabbit
with a pocket watch.

"Whoever heard of a rabbit with a pocket – or a watch?" thought Alice curiously...

...and she followed him
down
    into
        his
            hole.

D
o
w
n
D
o
w
n
D
o
w
n

Alice thought the hole would
never end, until she landed —
with a BUMP.

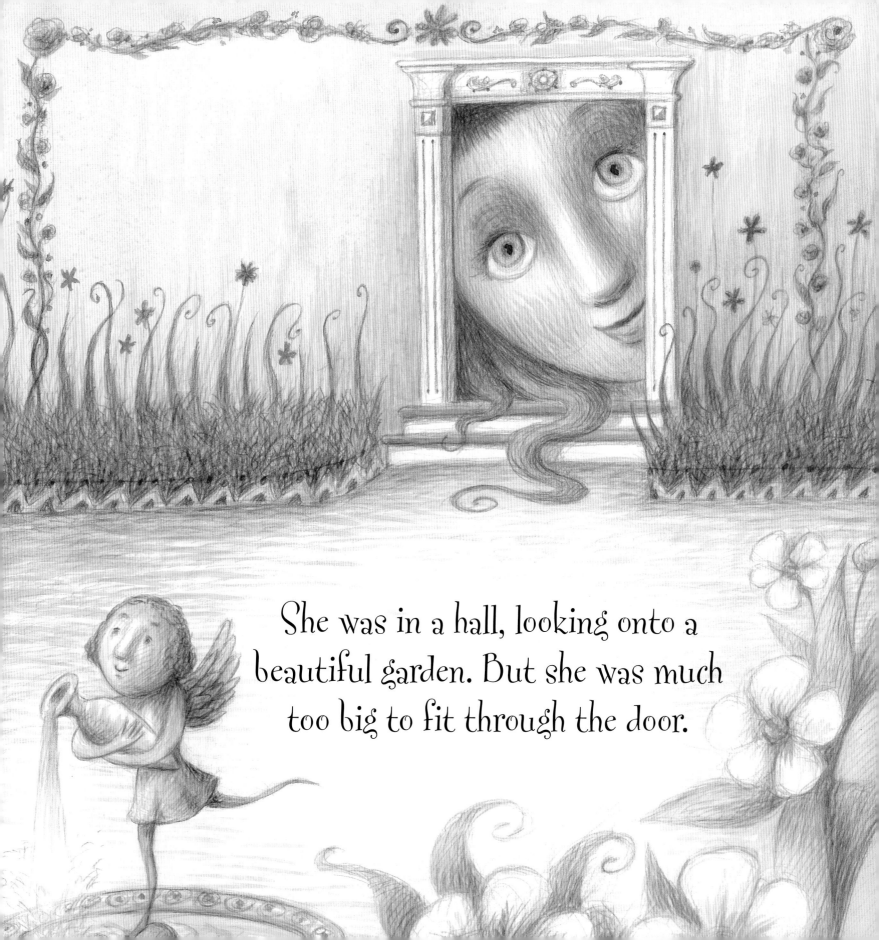

She was in a hall, looking onto a beautiful garden. But she was much too big to fit through the door.

Sunlight glinted on a glass bottle in the hall.

"Falling down holes is thirsty work,"
thought Alice. She took a great big gulp...

...and shrank to the size of a mouse.
Now she could fit through the door!

She was walking past a curly table leg
when she saw an
inviting cake.

"Eat me!"
it said.

Eat Me

Alice bit into the sticky icing... and shot up so quickly, her head hit the ceiling.

Now she was much too tall.

Alice started to cry.

Huge, salty tears splashed onto the floor.

Just then, the White Rabbit ran past in a fluster.

"Oh my ears and whiskers,
I'll be late!"

he gasped, dropping his fan.

Alice scooped it up...
and shrank again.

With a *splish* she tumbled into her salty lake of tears.

Peculiar creatures crowded around her.

"Swim for the shore!" they cried, so Alice swam.

"Shall I tell you a story?" she said, as they dried off. "My cat—"

"CAT?" they squawked and hurried away in a scurry of claws and a flurry of wings.

Left all alone, Alice wandered along until she met a grumpy-looking caterpillar.

"Who are you?" he said.

"I don't know," sighed Alice. "I keep growing and shrinking and it's all very confusing."

"Try eating some of my mushroom," said the caterpillar.

Alice nibbled a piece.

In a blink, the caterpillar vanished and a grinning cat appeared. Alice was baffled – and totally lost. "Where do I go now?" she asked.

"*That* way for the Hatter and *that* way for the March Hare," said the cat.

Alice decided to visit the Hare and found the Hatter there too. They were drinking tea and talking nonsense.

"Why is a raven like a writing desk?"

Alice got more and more confused.

"This is the stupidest tea party ever!" she said, running off.

"What party? Who are you?" snapped a voice. Alice had run slap-bang-wham into the Queen of Hearts.

"We're about to play a game," said the King, before
Alice could answer. "Won't you join us?"

It was the strangest game
Alice had ever seen.

Anyone who played badly was dragged away by the Queen's guards.

"Everyone to court!" said the Queen, all of a sudden.
Alice followed behind but she was growing again.
"Off with her head!" shouted the Queen.

"Nonsense!" said Alice.

"You're nothing but a pack of cards!" she added.

Suddenly, everything whirled into the air,
spinning her around, faster and faster.

Alice shut her
eyes tight.

When she opened them again, all the cards had gone...
and she was back at the top of the rabbit hole.

Edited by Jenny Tyler
Designed by Katarina Dragoslovic
Cover design by Russell Punter

First published in 2006 by Usborne Publishing Ltd, 83-85 Saffron Hill, London EC1N 8RT, England.
www.usborne.com Copyright © 2006 Usborne Publishing Ltd. The name Usborne and the devices ♀ ⊕are Trade Marks
of Usborne Publishing Ltd. All rights reserved. No part of this publication may be reproduced, stored in a retrieval system,
or transmitted in any form or by any means, electronic, mechanical, photocopying, recording or otherwise,
without the prior permission of the publisher. First published in America in 2007. UE. Printed in Dubai.